W9-AGM-249

Kylie Jean

Hoop Queen

by Marci Peschke

illustrated by Tuesday Mourning

PICTURE WINDOW BOOKS
a capstone imprint

Kylie Jean is published by Picture Window Books
A Capstone Imprint
1710 Roe Crest Drive
North Mankato, Minnesota 56003
www.capstonepub.com

Library of Congress Cataloging-in-Publication Data
Peschke, M. (Marci)
  Hoop queen / by Marci Peschke ; illustrated by Tuesday Mourning.
      p. cm. — (Kylie Jean)
  ISBN 978-1-4048-5962-3 (library binding) — ISBN 978-1-4048-6617-1 (pbk.)
  [1. Basketball—Fiction. 2. Contests—Fiction. 3. Texas—Fiction.] I. Mourning, Tuesday,
ill. II. Title.
  PZ7.P441245Ho 2011
  [Fic]—dc22   2010030654

Summary: Kylie Jean is usually good at everything she tries. So how come learning to
play basketball is so hard?

Creative Director: Heather Kindseth
Graphic Designer: Emily Harris
Editor: Beth Brezenoff
Production Specialist: Michelle Biedscheid

Design Element Credit:
Shutterstock/blue67design

Printed and bound in China.
012017   010243R

For Cara Mia
With love for Rick

—M.P.

Table of Contents

All About Me, Kylie Jean!

My name is Kylie Jean Carter. I live in a big, sunny, yellow house on Peachtree Lane in Jacksonville, Texas with Momma, Daddy, and my two brothers, T.J. and Ugly Brother.

T.J. is my older brother, and Ugly Brother is . . . well . . . he's really a dog. Don't you go telling him he is a dog. Okay? I mean it. He thinks he is a real true person.

He is a black-and-white bulldog. His front looks like his back, all smashed in. His face is all droopy like he's sad, but he's not.

His two front teeth stick out, and his tongue hangs down. (Now you know why his name is Ugly Brother.)

Everyone I love to the moon and back lives in Jacksonville. Nanny, Pa, Granny, Pappy, my aunts, my uncles, and my cousins all live here. I'm extra lucky, because I can see all of them any time I want to!

My momma says I'm pretty. She says I have eyes as blue as the summer sky and a smile as sweet as an angel. (Momma says pretty is as pretty does. That means being nice to the old folks, taking care of little animals, and respecting my momma and daddy.)

But I'm pretty on the outside and on the inside. My hair is long, brown, and curly.

I wear it in a ponytail sometimes, but my absolute most favorite is when Momma pulls it back in a princess style on special days.

I just gave you a little hint about my big dream. Ever since I was a bitty baby I have wanted to be an honest-to-goodness beauty queen. I even know the wave. It's side to side, nice and slow, with a dazzling smile. I practice all the time, because everybody knows beauty queens need to have a perfect wave.

I'm Kylie Jean, and I'm going to be a beauty queen. Just you wait and see!

Chapter One
Little Dribblers

It's a warm fall day right after school. Even from inside my house, I can hear the thump thump thump of T.J.'s basketball beating the driveway as he dribbles. Suddenly it stops, and I can imagine the ball going SWOOSH right through the net.

I decide to go outside and watch T.J. Grabbing a cookie and a juice box, I head out the door. Ugly Brother follows me. We sit down beside the driveway on the grass.

"Hey, lil' bit. What's up?" T.J. asks.

"Nothin' much," I reply. I sip my juice box with a loud slurp.

Bounce, bounce, bounce. The orange ball hops across the driveway and stops right in front of my feet.

"Hey. Come shoot some baskets with me," T.J. says.

I turn around and look behind me. Maybe he's talking to someone else. But no one's there.

"Me?" I ask.

T.J. rolls his eyes. "No. Ugly Brother," he says. "Of course you. Come on!"

Just then, Daddy's truck pulls into the driveway. He honks his horn twice.

T.J. picks up the basketball and drags me away from the driveway so that Daddy can park.

Daddy takes off his jacket and tie as soon as he gets out of the truck. "Let's shoot some hoops!" he hollers.

T.J. smiles. "You're on!" he says. "I was tryin' to get Kylie Jean to play, too."

"I'll play," I say.

My brother throws the ball right through the net. Swoosh! Turning to me, he says, "I already asked you to play, and you didn't even want to. Now you do, just because Dad's playing."

"Yup," I say. I grin.

Daddy laughs his big laugh and tosses me the ball. My arms are out, and I jump up to catch it.

Pow! It hits me
right in the stomach.

Boom! I land right
on my rear end.

Daddy and T.J.
run over. Ugly
Brother just looks at
me. He's too lazy to get up.

"Are you okay, sweetheart?" Daddy asks,
kneeling down next to me. "I'm so sorry! Why
didn't you catch the ball?"

"I don't know how to play basketball, Daddy!"
I say.

"You need some lessons, that's all," he says.
"Then you'll be fantastic!"

T.J. gives me a hand and pulls me up. "I've been watchin' it," I say. "But I don't understand it very much. Maybe playin' would help me more."

"She'll need a team and a coach," T.J. says. "Don't look at me, 'cause I'm not teaching her." T.J. is busy most days. He has practice with his varsity team and games on Friday nights at the high school.

Daddy ignores him and smiles. "I've got two words for you, Kylie Jean. Little Dribblers."

"What's that?" I ask.

T.J. rolls his eyes again. He says when he was my age, he was a Little Dribbler. Now Daddy and T.J. are slapping each other on the back and talking about the good old days when he was in second grade.

"Hello! What about me?" I shout.

Daddy kisses the top of my head. "You're going to learn to play basketball on a Little Dribblers team. I'll sign you up tomorrow," he tells me. Then he asks, "You do want to learn, right?"

I raise my hand to give him a high-five. Slap slap and just like that, I'm gonna be a basketball player!

Chapter Two
The Coach

The next day, Daddy picks me up from school. We go straight to the Jacksonville Recreation Center to sign up for Little Dribblers.

When we get inside it smells like sweat and swimming pools. It's crowded! Moms and dads and boys and girls are everywhere.

Daddy holds my hand. He says, "Stick with me, baby girl."

"I plan to, Daddy," I say. "I don't want to get lost in here!"

Then I see my friend Cara. "Hey, Cara!" I shout. "Daddy, that's my friend!" I tell my dad.

Cara runs over and we hug. "Are you going to be a Little Dribbler?" she asks.

"I guess so," I say. "Daddy really wants me to."

Daddy shakes his head. "Kylie Jean, don't do this just to make me happy," he tells me. "Do it because you want to learn the game."

"I do want to," I say.

"It's fun," Cara tells me. "You'll love it."

Just then, a poster catches my eye. It says: "Are you the next Little Dribbler King or Queen?"

I start to feel all wiggly inside. After all, my true dream is to be a beauty queen.

Cara sees me looking at the sign. "They have that queen stuff every year," she tells me. "People give money for every basket you make at the Free Throw Tournament. Whoever makes the most money and the most baskets is the Queen or the King. Then they let you give the money to help sick people or something like that."

"Are you telling me that all I have to do is get some money and I'll be the queen?" I blurt out, amazed. "And I can help people, too?"

"Uh huh," Cara says. "If you make the baskets."

The line starts moving. Daddy and I still hold hands as we move up the line, too. My free hand is just itching to do the beauty queen wave, nice and slow, side to side.

Instead, I shove it in my pocket and pull out some Bit-O-Honey candy to chew on. I pass Cara a piece, too. Beauty queens always share.

At the front of the line, we run into big trouble. The lady behind the table is wearing a striped sweatshirt and carrying a clipboard. "I'm sorry," she tells Daddy. "We just have more girls who want to play basketball than we have coaches."

Daddy looks sad. "I guess that means no basketball for you this year, peanut," he tells me. "Maybe next year."

The lady says, "You know, she can go on the waiting list. If anyone quits, we'll call you."

"Can't you just add more coaches?" Daddy asks. "Then more girls can play."

The striped-shirt lady laughs. "I'd love to, sugar," she says. "Problem is, we just don't have the coaches."

"Let me take care of that," Daddy says. He's smiling. I guess he's not worried about it, but I still am!

Daddy winks at me. Then he tells the lady to go ahead and put my name on the reserve list. "I have someone in mind," he says.

"Who?" I ask. But Daddy just winks again and starts pulling me toward the door.

I wave goodbye to Cara. Then Daddy and I head out to the parking lot.

Once we get in the truck, I buckle my seat belt, scowl, and cross my arms. "Are you going to tell me what's going on?" I demand.

Daddy laughs. "You're going to love your new coach," he says. "If we ask him the right way, I know he'll do it."

I ask, "What's the right way to ask?"

"You have to be the one to ask," Daddy says. "If anyone else did, it wouldn't work."

I throw up my hands. "I would, if I knew who it was!" I say.

Right then, we pull into Granny and Pappy's driveway. Pappy is outside, polishing one of his cars. Daddy parks the car and looks at me. "Do you know who it is now?" he asks.

I nod. Then I get out of the car as quick as lightning. I run over and tug on Pappy's shirt.

"Well, hello, princess!" Pappy says. "What brings you here?"

"I need your help awful bad, so pretty please say yes," I tell him.

"Slow down, darlin'," Pappy says. "Now, just what do you need, Kylie Jean?"

Daddy is standing back, watching. I give Pappy a big squeezy hug.

"I was just wonderin' if you would be my new basketball coach," I say, crossing my fingers behind my back for good luck.

Pappy grins real big. "Huh. Little Dribblers?" he asks.

"That's right!" I say.

"Well, I guess I can. I coached your daddy when he was a boy," Pappy says, pointing at Daddy. "And if I can teach him," he adds with a wink, "I can teach anybody."

I jump up and down with joy, shouting, "Thank you, thank you! You're the best pappy in the whole wide world!"

Chapter Three
We Are the Honey Bees

The next Saturday morning, we have our first practice. I wear pink shorts and a pink top that has a sparkly crown on the front. Pink is my color.

When I'm all ready, Daddy drops me off at the high school gym. Pappy is already there. So are a whole bunch of girls.

When Pappy sees me, he blows his whistle. "Well, aren't you just the bee's knees!" he shouts. "Come over here and give your pappy a hug."

I run over and hug him. "Do bees have knees?" I ask.

"No, they don't," Pappy admits. "That just means you're cute. No one looks at sweet in pink as you do, Kylie Jean."

I do a quick twirl around and say, "Thank you, Pappy!"

Then Cara walks in. "Hey, Kylie Jean!" she yells. Some of our other friends come in too. Kristy, Paula, Katie, and my cousin Lucy are all going to be on my team! Basketball practice is going to be fun. But I know it'll also be a lot of hard work.

Soon, our whole team is there. Ten girls stand in a circle around Pappy. He announces, "Since this is our first practice, we need to choose a name! Any ideas, girls?"

Lucy raises her hand. "I like the name Angels," she says.

You know me — I'm trying to think of a name with "pink" or "princesses" or something like that in it.

"I like the Pink Panthers, but that sounds like a movie," I say.

"It *is* a movie!" Cara shouts. "Think of another name."

We keep calling out names. Pappy is trying to write all of them down. He has to write real fast to keep up with all of us.

"Diamonds!"

"Flower Power!"

"Dunking Divas!"

Suddenly, an idea hits my brain like a score on a board! "Let's be the Honey Bees!" I yell.

I can already imagine our fans chanting.

"Buzz buzz buzz! Our Bees are the best! As sweet as honey, they pass the test!"

"Honey Bees, Honey Bees, goooooooooo Honey Bees!"

Everyone cheers. They like it! Pappy gives me a high five. "Super!" he says.

My team is buzzing about being Honey Bees. Yay!

Chapter Four
Drills and Thrills

Now that we have a name, we get down to business.

First, we all line up and run drills. That means we have to run to one side of the gym, touch a painted line on the floor, and then run back again. Running is good. I know how to run already.

Next, Coach Pappy teaches us how to dribble the ball.

I hold the ball like a giant orange in my hand. Then I bounce it hard on the gym floor.

It's supposed to bounce back up so I can do it all again, but my ball flies back up over my head. Then it rolls across the floor and I have to chase it.

Cara is a super dribbler. Bounce, bounce, bounce, she dribbles around the court.

"How did you learn to dribble so good?" I ask.

Cara laughs. "Think about jumping rope," she tells me. "Dribbling is just like that. Once you get your bounce going, you're buzzing!"

My trouble is, I can't seem to get my bounce going. Even Lucy seems to be able to dribble a little without the ball running away from her.

I sit down on the gym floor and watch my team. All of the Honey Bees can dribble a little bit. Yep, every Bee except me!

Pappy comes over and pats me on the head. "You can't let the ball beat you," he says. "Just get up and show that ball you're the boss."

"Can you help me?" I ask quietly.

Pappy smiles. "Sure thing, sugar," he says. "I can help you find your bounce."

Then he puts his hand over mine, and we do the double dribble. Bounce, bounce, bounce.

The ball moves across the floor. Pappy lets go.

Bounce, bounce, bounce. The ball slips to the side and tries to sneak away, but I follow it. With my right hand, I take charge.

I slap that basketball right back down on the court!

I've got it! I'm happier than a bee in honey.

Just wait until I tell Daddy. I'm a dribbler! A real, true, little dribbler!

Practice is almost over. Pappy blows his whistle twice.

"Gather 'round, little Bees!" he shouts. "Next time we practice, we're going to work on shooting baskets. You all have to get ready for the Free Throw Tournament!"

"What's that?" Lucy asks nervously.

Pappy smiles at her. "In a few weeks, there's a big contest," he says. "Whoever shoots the most free throws wins. But it's not just about winning. Before the tournament, you make a pledge sheet, and ask people to pledge money."

"What's pledging?" I ask.

"That's when people promise they'll give a dollar — or a quarter or a nickel — for every basket you make," Pappy explains. "Then you give that money to a charity. And whoever makes the most money wins the title of Little Dribbler Queen."

"The boys do it, too," Cara says. "Only one of them turns out to be the King."

"That's right," Pappy says, nodding.

"So winning isn't just about getting the most people to donate money. You also have to be good at shooting baskets. You have to have both to win. Get it?"

I nod. I get it. But now I'm a little nervous.

I'm not a good dribbler. What if I'm not a good basket-shooter either? What if I can't win the prize? What if I get lots of people to pledge, but I don't make any baskets? This isn't going to be as easy as I thought.

Chapter Five
Doggies

Ugly Brother is waiting for me by the front door when Pappy drops me off after practice. I bend down and kiss him on the head.

"I dribbled the ball at practice," I tell him, scratching behind his ears the way he likes. "You should have been there. I was awesome!"

We go into the house. I can hear the T.V. on in the den and T.J.'s loud music coming from his room upstairs.

Momma calls, "Kylie Jean, is that you?"

"Yup, it's me," I holler back. "I'm a little dribbler and a Honey Bee!"

I follow Momma's voice and the smell of fresh brownies to the kitchen. I hop onto a stool and sniff the air.

"Yum-o!" I say. "It sure smells chocolatey in here." Then I notice a big piece of pink paper on the counter. "Momma, can I have that pink piece of paper?" I ask.

"What for?" Momma asks.

"For making my pledge sheet," I explain. "I have to get people to promise to give me money if I make baskets at the Free Throw Tournament. Then I give that money to charity."

Momma smiles. "Of course you can have the paper," she tells me. "What charity are you going to donate your money to?"

I look at Momma. I haven't even thought of who to give my money to! "I don't know," I admit. "I'll have to think about it."

I grab the paper and run up to my room to decorate it. Ugly Brother follows me upstairs. What I need is a decorating plan for my paper. Right?

I'm thinking pink. You know I just love that color! Some gold glitter would be very nice, too.

While I get out my art supplies, Ugly Brother curls up next to my bed and starts to take a snooze. Looking at Ugly Brother, I get an idea that's sweeter than honey.

I'm going to use the money I get for shooting baskets to help little doggies that have no place to live!

"Momma!" I yell. "Come quick!"

A minute later, Momma bursts into my room. "Are you okay? What's wrong?" she says.

"I'm okay," I say. "I just wanted to tell you I picked out my charity!"

Momma lets out a loud breath like she went for a jog or something. "Oh, Kylie Jean, you scared me half to death," she says. She shakes her head. "What's the charity?"

"A dog one," I say. "Can you help me figure out a good place to give my money to that helps dogs?"

Momma smiles. "Yes, I can," she says. "But next time, please don't yell for me like that. I thought you set your room on fire!"

Silly Momma. I would never do that! I like the stuff in my room too much.

Momma leaves. Then I get busy.

I cut. I glue. I sprinkle glitter.

Finally, I show Ugly Brother my pledge sheet.

It has the cutest little doggy face on the front. The doggy is wearing a gold glitter crown. Underneath the doggy are the lines for people to write in their pledges.

They will write their names and then how much they want to give me for each basket.

Ugly Brother bends his head to one side and then the other. He is deciding whether he likes it or not.

I tape the sheet to my wall so that I can admire it. "You like it, don't you?" I ask Ugly Brother. Ugly Brother barks twice. That means yes!

I bring my pledge sheet to dinner. Daddy and T.J. are setting the table while Momma finishes cooking the chicken.

"What do you have there?" Daddy asks.

I show him the pink decorated paper. "It's my pledge sheet," I explain. "For the Free Throw Tournament."

T.J. laughs. "You think you're gonna make any baskets?" he asks meanly. "No way. You can't even dribble."

Daddy glares at T.J. "I'm going to pledge a dollar per basket," Daddy tells me.

Then T.J.'s face turns red. "You only pledged fifty cents for me when I was a Little Dribbler!" he says.

"And I was going to give Kylie Jean fifty cents, too," Daddy says. "But your comment made me change my mind. Now, how much are you going to pledge for your sister?"

T.J. frowns. "You can put me down for a quarter for each basket," he finally tells me. I can see that he wants to make another mean comment, but Daddy gives him a look.

That night, sleep is not my
friend. Too many thoughts
are in my head, thoughts
about dribbling, shooting
baskets, and about my
pretty pink paper with the
cutest little doggy.

Even when I finally fall
asleep, I dream about basketball.
In my dream, the Honey Bees are playing against
the Giants, and I score the winning basket.

* * *

On Sunday, I take my pledge sheet along
with me to church. After the service, while the
grownups stand around and drink coffee, I move
sweetly from group to group.

I show them my pledge sheet and tell them all about the doggies I want to help.

Four people decide to make pledges. A lot of people want to, but they already made pledges to other kids. I guess that's okay, since everyone's money is going to help someone.

In the car on the way to Nanny and Pa's farm after church, I study my pledge sheet. I don't really get it.

"Did you get a lot of pledges?" T.J. asks, peeking over at my pledge sheet. He's trying to be nicer to me today.

"I got four," I tell him. "But I still don't get it. If I make baskets, how much money will I get for the dogs?"

T.J. takes my sheet and looks it over. "Daddy pledged a dollar, and I pledged a quarter," he says. "And the people at church pledged a total of two dollars. So that's three dollars and a quarter for each basket."

"So how much is it if I make ten baskets?" I ask.

T.J. thinks a second. "That would make it about thirty-two dollars and fifty cents," he says. "That's pretty good, Kylie Jean!"

I smile. "How much money did the Little Dribbler Queen earn when you did the Free Throw Tournament?" I ask.

T.J. glances up at Daddy in the rear-view mirror. Then he says, "I don't know if you want to hear this, Kylie Jean."

"Oh, just tell me," I say. Daddy turns the van down Nanny and Pa's dirt road.

"Okay," T.J. says. He takes a deep breath and says, "She earned more than three hundred dollars."

I sit back in my seat, shocked. "You better not be messin' with me," I say quietly.

T.J. shakes his head. "I'm not, Kylie Jean, I swear," he says.

"Did she make a whole bunch of baskets, or did she get a lot of people to pledge money?" I ask. I notice that Momma and Daddy are quiet, listening to us talk.

T.J. shrugs. "Both," he says. "That's the whole point. You have to do both to win."

Daddy parks the car at Nanny and Pa's house. I hop out. I'm hoping the people in my family will pledge some money. Otherwise there's no way I'll win Little Dribbler Queen — and I won't be able to help those doggies.

Chapter Six
Susie's News

On Monday morning, I gobble up two Pop Tarts and gulp my milk. When the bus comes to take me to school, I want to be waiting out front. Our bus driver, Mr. Jim, is my friend.

As soon as I hop up the steps to the bus, I push my pledge sheet up to Mr. Jim's face. I want him to be able to see it real good.

I tell him all about the Little Dribblers, and the queen, and the doggies that need help.

Mr. Jim listens. He's a good listener. "All right," he says when he's finished. "I'll pledge twenty-five cents for every basket you make, Kylie Jean."

"Thank you!" I say, smiling.

"But which animal shelter are you donating your money to?" he asks.

I shrug. "I don't know yet," I tell him.

"Think about donating to Places for Pups," he says. "That's where I got my dog, Jasper. They're a real good place, and they need the money."

"Places for Pups," I say. "That sounds good!"

Mr. Jim writes down his pledge on my sheet. "Now sit down," he tells me. "And don't tell anyone else I pledged money for you. Or they'll all want money."

"You got it!" I whisper, giving him a wink. Then I skip back to an empty seat.

Mr. Jim is the best bus driver in the whole wide world. While he drives us toward school, stopping to pick up kids on our way, I wonder who else is trying to be the Little Dribbler Queen.

I don't have to wonder too long. Three stops after mine, we pick up Susannah. Susie is nice. She is carrying a big piece of paper. It has pretty flowers all over it. I like it.

"Hey, are you saving that seat?" she asks me.

"Yup," I say. "For you!"

Susie sits down right next to me. She starts telling me all about her Little Dribbler team, the Shooting Stars.

"We are having so much fun!" she says.

"The Honey Bees are having fun, too," I tell her. "I like it, so far."

"What kind of uniforms did you guys get?" Susie asks.

I frown. "What do you mean?" I ask. "We don't have uniforms. We just wear shorts and T-shirts!"

"We have brand-new blue and gold uniforms," Susie tells me. "You won't believe it, but Taco U.S.A. paid for our uniforms! They say Taco U.S.A. on the back. I love them!"

"Why did they pay for your uniforms?" I ask.

Susie shrugs. "I guess so that people would see that they're nice," she says. "Our coach said it means we're sponsored. It makes me feel like I'm in a commercial!"

I like the sound of that! I will have to ask Pappy about getting sponsored.

"Are you doing the Free Throw Tournament?" Susie asks me.

I scrunch up my face. "Yes," I tell her. "But I'm not sure I'll be very good at free throws."

"All the money I make in the tournament is going to the Grace Food Bank," she says.

"What's a food bank?" I ask. "A place where you keep food safe? We don't have one of those. We just have a refrigerator."

Susie laughs. "No. A food bank isn't for keeping food safe, silly," she says. "People with no food can go there and grocery shop for free."

"That's awesome!" I say.

Susie says, "That's why I'm giving them my money."

I tell her all about giving my money to Places for Pups. You know, it gives me a thrill, helping people and pooches. It is almost as exciting as being a queen. Almost . . .

Chapter Seven
First Free Throw

On Saturday morning, the gym smells like
T.J.'s dirty socks. It's warm in here, too, probably
because we have been running around so much
chasing basketballs.

We have been working on free throws. Here is
how you shoot a free throw.

You stand at the line painted on the basketball
court floor. You hold the ball carefully so that you
don't drop it. Then you can dribble it in place for a
second if you want to. I am too scared I'll lose the
ball, so I don't dribble.

You look up at the hoop. You take a deep breath. Then you jump up and throw the ball at the same time.

If your name is Kylie Jean Carter, the ball does not go in the hoop.

I am not kidding. I try a hundred times. Every single time, the ball flies too high, or too low, or off to the side. One time it almost hits Cara! But it doesn't go through the hoop even once.

After a while, I give up. I sit down on a bleacher on the side of the gym and watch the Honey Bees practice. Everyone makes some free throws. Even Lucy.

Pappy notices that I'm sitting down. He walks over and sits down on the bleacher next to me. "What's wrong, puddin'?" he asks. "Are you hurt?"

I shake my head. "No sir," I say. "But the fact is, I'm not so good at free throws." I sigh. "And that means I'm not gonna be the Little Dribbler Queen, and I'm not gonna help save those doggies."

Pappy frowns. "I'm disappointed in you, little miss," he says.

"Because I can't make free throws?" I ask, staring sadly down at my feet.

"No, Kylie Jean," Pappy says quietly. "Because it's not like you to give up."

Pappy is right. So I tell him so. "You're right, Pappy," I say. "Could you please help me with my free throws?"

"Of course," Pappy says, standing up. "Let's get to work."

Pappy and I practice free throws for a while at one end of the gym while the other Honey Bees practice at the other side. I miss the first three shots, and I want to give up, but I know I can't. Those sad doggies need me. So I keep trying.

I stand. I look at the basket. I jump and throw the ball.

And it goes in!

The gym fills with cheers. I turn around and see the rest of my team clapping and smiling. "You did it, Kylie Jean!" Cara says. "Good job!"

"Thank you," I say, smiling.

Pappy checks his watch. Practice is almost over. He says, "Let's talk, girls. Next week, we'll play our first game against another team. We'll be playing against the Shooting Stars."

That makes me think of what Susie told me. I raise my hand.

"Coach Pappy," I say, "did you know that the Shooting Stars have real uniforms?" Some of the other girls gasp.

Pappy looks sad. "I do know that," he says. "But uniforms cost money."

"Leave it to me, Pappy," I tell him. "I think I know who we can ask for new uniforms."

"Honey Bees," I holler, "we're gonna get some new uniforms. You just wait and see."

* * *

At supper that night, I put my fork down and look at Daddy. "Daddy, I have a question to ask you," I say.

"Go right ahead," Daddy says, smiling. He winks at Momma.

"I would like to know if I can come to your job on Monday," I tell him. "I was thinkin' maybe some people at the newspaper might like animals, and maybe they would pledge some money for my Free Throw Tournament."

T.J. laughs. "I thought you couldn't make free throws or dribble," he says.

"That's not true at all," I say. "In fact, I dribbled and made a free throw just this morning."

I turn away from T.J. I'm not going to listen to him if he's going to be mean to me!

"I think it would be just fine if you came by my office," Daddy says. "I'll pick you up from school on Monday and bring you in. Sound good, sugar drop?"

"Thanks, Daddy!" I say. I give him my best beauty queen smile. The first part of my plan is done!

Chapter Eight
Miss Laura

As soon as the bell rings after school on Monday, I race outside. Just like he promised, Daddy's car is waiting next to the buses. I run over and hop into the backseat.

"Hey there, sugar," Daddy says. "You ready to go to my office?"

I nod and buckle my seatbelt. "Yes sir," I tell him. I hold up my pledge sheet. "I just know everybody you work with is going to want to pledge me some money for those sad, lonely doggies."

Daddy laughs while he drives away. "I hope so, sweetheart. Well, I told them all you're coming, and they're real excited to meet you," he says.

Daddy's office is on Main Street. It's right next door to a post office and across from a place where Momma goes to pick up Daddy's shirts sometimes. He parks the car in front and opens my door for me.

We hold hands as we walk through the front door of Daddy's office. A bell jingles as the door opens. The lady at the front desk looks up and smiles at me. "You must be Kylie Jean," she says.

"That's right, Mary," Daddy says. "This is my little princess."

I give Mary my best beauty queen wave, nice and slow, side to side.

Then I ask, "Do you like animals?"

"I sure do," Mary tells me.

"Would you like to pledge money for the Little Dribbler Free Throw Tournament?" I ask. "All you have to do is sign up on my pretty pledge sheet." I show her the sheet. "You can pledge any money you want, and then you give me the money for each free throw I make," I explain.

Mary smiles again. "I'd love to, dear," she says. "I'll give you a dime for every free throw."

"Thank you!" I say. "You're so nice!"

Daddy leads me through the office. Everyone there is as busy as a bee! He introduces me to a lot of people he works with. Some people pledge money. Some people don't.

One lady told me that she already pledged fifty cents a basket to her niece. "That's okay," I tell her. "That's real nice of you anyway!"

Finally, Daddy turns to me and says, "I think that's everyone, puddin' pop. You've gotten a lot of pledges."

I frown. "But Daddy," I say, "I didn't talk to everyone."

"Who else did you want to talk to?" Daddy asks, smiling.

"Miss Laura!" I tell him.

Miss Laura is Daddy's boss. She has a big office with a window that looks out onto Main Street. She is very busy. Her office is full of papers. But I need to talk to her. It's the second part of my plan!

Daddy shakes his head. "Miss Laura is too busy," he tells me. "But I can ask her tomorrow if she'd like to give you a pledge."

"Okay," I say slowly. "Can I go to the bathroom?"

"Go ahead," Daddy says. "It's down the hall." He points down the office hall to a door with a sign that says WOMEN.

I skip down the hall and go into the bathroom. Before I close the door, I peek back. Daddy has turned around. He's talking to someone. So I sneak out of the bathroom and run! I go down the hall and turn the corner.

Soon I'm standing outside Miss Laura's office. I can hear her talking, but no one else, so she must be on the phone.

After a few seconds, she stops talking. I hear a clicking noise. It sounds just like when T.J. is typing on his computer.

Then I hear something else. Daddy's voice! It's coming closer. So I quickly knock on the door.

"Come in," Miss Laura's voice says.

I open the door and walk in. Miss Laura is sitting behind a big wooden desk. She frowns for a second, but then she smiles. "You're Kylie Jean Carter, aren't you?" she asks.

I nod. "Yes ma'am," I say.

"Are you looking for your daddy, sweetheart?" Miss Laura asks. She starts to get up.

"No, ma'am," I say. "I'm here on official business."

Miss Laura raises her eyebrows. Then she sits down at her desk again. "In that case, please have a seat," she says. "How can I help you?"

I sit down. "Ma'am, do you like to play basketball?" I ask.

She smiles. "I did when I was your age," she tells me. "In fact, I was a Little Dribbler right here in town."

My eyes get really wide. "You were?" I whisper. "I'm a Little Dribbler!"

"I loved it," she says. "Do you like being a Little Dribbler?"

"Yes ma'am," I say. "But I'm not very good. Anyway, that's why I'm here. My team needs uniforms. Right now we just wear shorts and T-shirts."

"I see," Miss Laura says.

Just then, I hear Daddy's voice. "Laura, I'm so sorry," he's saying. I look up as he walks into the room. "Kylie Jean, let's leave Miss Laura alone. She's got a lot of work to do."

"It's okay," Miss Laura says. She winks at me and adds, "Kylie Jean is here on official business."

Daddy frowns and looks at me. Then he looks at Miss Laura. She smiles and says, "Go on, Kylie Jean."

"Like I was saying, we play in shorts and T-shirts," I say. "But the Shooting Stars have fancy new blue and gold uniforms. And you know who bought them? Taco U.S.A.! They want people to think they're nice, and havin' girls wear their uniforms with the Taco U.S.A. name on the back is like a commercial."

"I see," Miss Laura says slowly. "Well, Kylie Jean, what does that have to do with me?"

"I was thinkin' that the newspaper could sponsor us!" I say. "Daddy's always sayin' that it's hard to get people to read the paper. Right, Daddy?"

I look up, and Daddy's face is red.

"Well," I go on, "if people see the name right on our backs during our games, they'll know y'all are real nice people! Then they'll want to read the paper."

Miss Laura laughs.

Daddy's face is still a little red. "I'm sorry, Laura," he says. "Kylie Jean, come on, now."

"No, no," Miss Laura says. "Kylie Jean, thank you for coming to see me. I think you'll make a very wise businesswoman someday."

"Thank you, ma'am," I say.

"How many girls are on your team?" she asks.

"There are ten of us," I tell her. "Cara, me, Lucy —"

Daddy interrupts me. "You don't need to tell her all the names, sweetheart."

"When is your first game?" Miss Laura asks, smiling at me.

"This Saturday is our first game," I tell her.

"What's your team's name?" she asks.

"We're the Honey Bees," I tell her.

"All right," Miss Laura says. "Your daddy and I will talk, and we'll order the uniforms for your team."

"Oh, thank you!" I cry. "Thank you, thank you, thank you!"

Chapter Nine
First Game

On Saturday morning, Daddy doesn't just drop me off at the gym. He parks the car and comes in with me. "Don't you have to go?" I ask.

Daddy smiles. "Nope. I have to check on something here first. And then I'm staying for your game!" he tells me.

I bite my lip. I'm really nervous about the game. I'm okay with dribbling now, but if I have to make a free throw, I don't know what will happen! I'm so nervous it feels like I swallowed some bees, and they are buzzing in my belly.

71

When we walk in, the first thing I see is Coach Pappy. He's standing in front of some big brown boxes.

"Oh, good!" Daddy says. "Looks like the delivery made it." He winks at me. Then he calls out, "How do they look, Pappy?"

Pappy smiles. He reaches into a box and pulls something out. It's a new basketball uniform!

The shirt is gold and pink, and the shorts are black. The front of the shirt says "Honey Bees" and has a picture of a bee. Each shirt has a girl's last name printed on the back, and a number, and it says the newspaper's name.

The best part of the uniform is the socks! They have black and gold stripes. Now we really will look like bees!

"They look wonderful!" I tell Daddy.

"Go try yours on," Daddy says.

Pappy blows his whistle, and everyone gathers around. He hands out shorts, a jersey, and a pair of socks to each girl. "Change in the locker room. See you back out here on the court for our game!" he says.

Before long, we're all dressed. Even from inside the locker room, I can hear the fans. It sounds like there are a lot of them!

"We're going to win!" Cara says.

Lucy moans. "I don't feel too good," she says quietly.

I pat her on the back. "You're just nervous," I tell her. "It'll be okay. We Bees have your back."

Lucy smiles a teeny tiny smile and nods her head.

Then we hear Coach Pappy blow the whistle two times. That means it's time to go play our very first game!

The Honey Bees run out to the gym. It is packed full of people. The bleachers on both sides look like walls made out of faces. Now I'm feeling jittery, too.

I look up into the stands. At first, I feel dizzy. Maybe joining the basketball team was a bad idea!

Then I see my bus driver, Mr. Jim, so I wave. He waves back.

Then I see Ms. Clarabelle, our neighbor, so I wave nice and slow, side to side, my beauty queen wave. She waves back.

Then I see my family. Everyone but Pappy is sitting in the very front row. I blow them all kisses. They are my fans.

Uncle Bay holds up a sign that says, "Go Smiley Kylie!" T.J. waves. Daddy gives me two thumbs-up. I sure wish Ugly Brother could see my first game, but they don't allow dogs in the gym, so I'll have to tell him all about it later.

I grab Lucy's hand, and we run out to the middle of the basketball court together. The other team is already out there.

We're supposed to try to beat each other, but we like those girls, so we hug and give each other high-fives.

Finally, the referee blows his whistle and motions for our teams to go to opposite ends of the court. He is sort of the boss of the game. I can tell you one thing: I sure don't want to get on his bad side.

Cara is the tallest girl on our team, so she walks to the center of the court for the tip-off. The referee will throw the ball up in the air. One girl from each team will stand in the middle of the court and try to slam that jump ball over to her team.

We all get ready to play. The whistle blows, Cara jumps, and the ball flies in our direction. Then we're all running around like crazy!

I keep getting confused. We run to their end of the court. Susie has the ball. I wave my hands in front of her, so she can't shoot. That's my job.

She tries to shoot, but the ball bounces off the hoop. I get it and dribble back to our end of the court. Then the game goes on.

At the end of the first quarter, we have two points, thanks to Cara. The other team has none. We still have three more quarters.

Coach Pappy pulls me and some girls out and puts other girls in the game. I'm glad to get pulled out. I want to rest on the bench and let some of the other girls play too. He leaves Cara in, because she's our best player.

The game starts up again. In the stands, Cara's daddy shouts, "That's my girl! You're open. Shoot!"

Swish! The ball goes through the net. The score is 4 to 0, and we are still winning. Then the Shooting Stars score. 4 to 2.

The teams move to our end of the court. Lucy throws the ball to Cara, but a player from the other team catches it. They dash down the court to the other basket, shoot the ball, and bam! We are tied 4 to 4.

No one scores during the third quarter. We're still tied when Coach Pappy puts me back in during the fourth quarter. It's almost the end of the game.

I pass the ball to Cara, and she makes her shot. The ball swirls around the rim of the basket and goes in.

Six to four, and the crowd goes wild!

Now it's the Stars' turn to move the ball to their end of the court. We run.

I try to get ahead of the girl who has the ball, but she's too fast this time. She shoots and scores.

Now we're tied again, 6 to 6. The game is almost over. We just can't lose now!

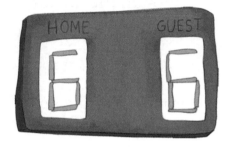

I have the ball, and I start dribbling toward our basket. Cara shouts, "Kylie Jean, pass to me!"

I look up.

She's pretty far away, but I might be able to make it. But I'm close to the basket. Thinking fast, I get ready to shoot.

This might be the shot that wins the game!

I tell myself, "You can do it!"

Daddy hollers, "Shoot, Kylie!"

I raise my arms, ready for that ball to go sailing through the air and win the game for the Bees. Then, suddenly, I'm kissing the wood floor. A girl from the Stars knocked me over just to keep me from making a basket!

A whistle blows. I just got fouled!

First, I'm a little mad. Then I'm worried. I have to make a free throw.

My feet feel like they're stuck to the floor. The ref keeps waving at me. Finally, he walks over and puts his hand on my shoulder. "You can shoot from the free throw line, honey," he says. "You can't shoot from here. Okay?"

I nod. I'm so scared that I'm going to miss the basket. But I follow the referee anyway.

I put my feet right at the edge of the white line. Then I look up. My whole family is standing up, waiting for me to shoot.

They start chanting, "Kylie Jean! Kylie Jean! Kylie Jean!"

"Okay, I'm ready now," I say.

The ref gives me the ball and steps back. The girls from the Shooting Stars are all in position. I close my eyes. Then, quick as lightning, I make the shot.

The ball flies through the air. It hits the basket and bounces away.

A girl on the Shooting Stars grabs the ball and dribbles down the court.

Just as the buzzer rings, she makes a basket.

The Stars win.

It's all my fault.

Chapter Ten
T.J.'s Special Shot

That night after supper, T.J. asks Daddy to shoot hoops with him. When they go out to the driveway, I find Ugly Brother in the living room, trying to take a nap. My dog snores really loud and grunts like a pig.

"Come on, Ugly Brother," I tell him. "You need to get some exercise." He doesn't move.

I pull on his collar a little bit. "I need you to help me with my free throw," I explain.

He opens one eye.

"If I stand on your back and throw the ball, I'll be tall enough to get it in the basket," I say.

He closes his eye.

"Don't you want to help all those sad doggies who don't have homes?" I ask, putting my hands on my hips.

Ugly Brother sighs. Then he gets up and walks to the front door.

Outside, I ask Daddy, "What's the score?"

"I'm ahead by two," he tells me. "It's 10 to 8."

Daddy makes one more basket. Then he says, "I have some work to finish up tonight. We'll have to play again later."

"Aw, man," T.J. complains. "No fair, Dad. I can beat you. Let's play for just a few more minutes."

"Sorry, son," Daddy says. He heads for the back door. T.J. drops down on the grass to cool off.

Now it's my turn. I push Ugly Brother over to the spot where the free-throw line usually goes. Then I get the basketball. Very carefully, I put one foot up on Ugly Brother's back, but I can't hold the ball and get my other foot up too. I am wobbling around like a baby who is trying to walk.

"Kylie Jean, you're gonna kill that dog!" T.J. says. "What are you trying to do?"

"You should help me, T.J.," I say. I explain all about my terrible free throw. T.J. nods like he understands. He gets up and walks over to me. Then he takes the ball and throws it.

Swish. It goes right in.

"Just tell me how to throw like that," I tell him. "Then I can be good and get points for my team." I don't add that I want to get some free throws in the Free Throw Tournament, too.

Dribbling the ball around the driveway, T.J. asks, "Do you think I always made baskets like that when I was your age?"

"I was a baby then," I say. "So I don't remember too much."

"You need to learn my special shot," T.J. tells me. "And then you have to practice it fifty times. No, make that a hundred times."

"Show me," I say.

He squats down, holding the ball. Then he jumps up, pushing the ball forward with all of his might.

The ball is going so fast and so far! It rattles the hoop as it slams into it. Then it slips through the net.

"Your turn," T.J. says.

I have to spread my feet far apart to hold the ball like T.J. did.

He's watching me. He shouts, "Jump and push the ball."

I do, but I miss.

"Try again," T.J. says.

The second time, the ball just barely touches the edge of the net.

I'm not going to give up.

This time, the ball soars up . . . up . . . and up.

Then it slowly travels down through the net and lands on the driveway.

T.J. cheers. "Way to go, Lil' Bit!" he says. "I knew you could do it. You just needed to learn my super special shot."

"T.J., you're the best," I say. "Thanks a lot for teaching me how to shoot."

"Keep working on it," T.J. says. "You remember what I told you, right?"

Ugly Brother looks at me, and I look at him.

"Wait a second," I say as T.J. walks toward the house. "Do I really have to shoot ninety-seven more times?"

He nods. And if you have a big brother, you know you have to do what they say!

Chapter Eleven
The Free Throw Tournament

Every day for the next week, I practice free throws. After school, I shoot free throws. After I finish my homework, I shoot free throws. After dinner, I shoot free throws.

At first, I'm not so good. On Monday, I shoot a hundred free throws and only make five of them!

But I keep trying. On Tuesday, I shoot a hundred free throws again. But this time, I make eleven of them.

On Wednesday, I work harder. I shoot a hundred and ten baskets. And I make twenty-five!

On Thursday, I shoot a hundred baskets. This time, I make forty of them.

On Friday, I decide I should rest my arms. I only shoot twenty-five baskets. But I make fifteen of them. That's more than half!

When I'm done shooting baskets, I stop by all of my neighbors' houses and ask them to pledge for the tournament.

Everyone gives me a pledge. Miss Clarabelle pledges a whole dollar for every single basket that I make!

I'm excited and nervous for Saturday. My tummy feels nervous, like there are a hundred little bees buzzing around in there.

On the day of the Free Throw Tournament, all of the Little Dribblers meet at the gym right away in the morning. "Good luck, puddin' pop," Daddy says as he drops me off. "You'll do great today."

"I hope so, Daddy," I say. "I truly do."

The Free Throw Tournament starts at 8 a.m. sharp. There are a lot of kids here. Boys and girls are in the gym, ready to make their best shots!

We each get ten minutes to make as many baskets as we can. There are four hoops in the gym, so four people shoot at one time. Cara, Lucy, Susie, and I are all shooting at the same time. We have about twenty minutes before it's our turn.

I look at my pledge sheet. A whole lot of people think I can make the baskets today.

Momma added it all up for me last night, and I'll make more than fifteen dollars for each basket! That's a whole lot of money for sad, lonely doggies.

And it could be enough to win. T.J. said the winner made three hundred dollars when he was a Little Dribbler. I do the math in my head. I'd have to make twenty baskets to make that much money.

I don't know if I can do it, but I sure hope so.

When it's my turn, I step up to the basket. There's a lady with a stopwatch and a piece of paper. She'll write down every basket I make. "Do you have your pledge sheet?" she asks.

I hand it to her. "Thanks. Let me know when you're ready," she says.

I squeeze my eyes tight and think about Ugly Brother. This money is for his friends, so that they never have to be lonely or hungry.

Then I look at the lady. "Okay," I say.

She pushes a button on the stopwatch. "Go!" she says.

I miss the first basket. But I make the second one, and the third. I miss the next one, but make three more after that. I can't believe it when the lady blows her whistle.

"Time's up!" she says.

"How many did I make, ma'am?" I ask.

She looks down at her paper.

I feel disappointed. I think I must have only made about ten baskets.

The lady counts the marks she made on her paper. "You made twenty-seven baskets!" she tells me.

Then she looks at my pledge sheet and her eyes get wide. "That's more than four hundred dollars!" she adds. "You did a great job!"

I smile wide. I only wanted to make twenty baskets so I could make three hundred dollars for those doggies. And I wasn't sure I'd be able to do it. But I did!

Yay! I am prouder than a mama hog with ten piglets.

Cara and Lucy run over to me. We share our scores. Cara made thirty-three baskets. She's a basketball star! And Lucy made sixteen.

We are all proud of how we did today. But I am still hoping I'll be the Little Dribbler Queen!

We eat snacks. We watch other kids shoot baskets.

Finally, a man turns on a microphone. He says, "If everyone will find a seat, we will announce this year's Little Dribbler Queen and King."

Cara and Lucy and I find a place to sit on one side of the gym. Out on the court, some boys T.J.'s age are moving a small platform into the center. Soon we will find out who the queen is. I sure hope it's me!

Some people are still coming in with nachos and hot dogs from the food stand in front of the gym. I am way too anxious to eat anything. I see Susie on the other side, and she waves to me.

I think about all the people she is trying to help at the Grace Food Bank. We have a lot of food to eat at our house. Momma probably has about a million cans in the pantry.

That makes us lucky. Susie is making some more people lucky today.

The lady who counted my baskets steps up onto the platform with a microphone. "I bet y'all want to know who our next Little Dribbler Queen and King are going to be. Right?" she asks us.

Everyone shouts, "Yes!" We are all getting antsy, and nobody wants to wait anymore to hear the winners. Especially me!

The lady talks some more about the history of the Little Dribbler King and Queen and all of the good things the past winners did with their money.

I tap my feet on the floor. They announce the Little Dribbler King. He made $350, and he's giving the money to some people who help make nice parks.

Then it's time to announce the Little Dribbler Queen.

"This year's winner made more than four hundred dollars!" the lady says. "In fact, that's a Little Dribblers record."

Please, let it be me! I think.

The lady smiles and says, "Kylie Jean Carter has collected $411.75 for Places for Pups and is our new Little Dribbler Queen."

I jump up! I don't run, because beauty queens don't run. Slowly, I walk to the platform.

"Congratulations, Kylie Jean! You are our new queen!" the lady exclaims.

Then she gives me a special basketball with a red ribbon tied around it and puts my new crown on my head. It is sparkly, with little orange stones in the shape of a basketball.

Holding my basketball, I turn and wave at the crowd nice and slow, side to side.

I see Pappy and all of the Honey Bees clapping for me.

That gives me a great idea! Then I take the microphone.

"Thank you!" I say. "I know a way you can all help some more. My friend Susie and I really want to help people and puppies, so if you could bring a can of people food or dog food to the next Little Dribbler game, you would make us real happy!"

I hand the microphone back. Susie runs up to me, and we hug. Then I show her the beauty queen wave, and we both turn and wave to the crowd nice and slow, and side to side. Everyone stands up, clapping and laughing and smiling. We are all happy.

Chapter Twelve
Me and Ugly Brother

At dinner, I tell my family all about my day. Daddy smiles when I finish my story. "You're the queen of the hoop, Kylie Jean," he says. "You did great today."

Momma adds, "I am so proud of you for thinking about asking the folks to bring canned goods. You are pretty inside and out. Pretty is as pretty does!" Then she kisses me on my cheek.

T.J. tells me not to get too big for my britches, but then he smiles. He says, "You're a pretty good kid, lil' bit."

After dinner, I cuddle with Ugly Brother in the big, cozy living room chair.

"Can you believe it?" I ask him. "We helped so many doggies today."

He barks, "Ruff, ruff." That means yes! Then he gives me lots of doggie kisses, because he is so proud of me.

Momma shouts, "Kylie Jean, get that dog off the furniture. You can tell him all about being the new queen of the hoop while he's sittin' on the floor."

Ugly Brother and I are too busy celebrating. I don't want him to get down.

"Oh, never mind," Momma says. "I guess it's okay for just tonight."

I'm glad she doesn't make him get down, because Ugly Brother and I are already thinking up a new plan for me to be a real true beauty queen!

Marci Bales Peschke was born in Indiana, grew up in Florida, and now lives in Texas with her husband, two children, and a feisty black and white cat named Phoebe. She loves reading and watching movies.

When **Tuesday Mourning** was a little girl, she knew she wanted to be an artist when she grew up. Now, she is an illustrator who lives in South Pasadena, CA. She especially loves illustrating books for kids and teenagers. When she isn't illustrating, Tuesday loves spending time with her husband, who is an actor, and their two sons.

Glossary

basket (BASS-kit), **hoop** (HOOP), **rim** (RIM)—words for the round, metal hole from which the net hangs in a basketball game

court (KORT)—the place where a game is played

dribble (DRIH-buhl)—to bounce a basketball using one hand

food bank (FOOD BANK)—a place where people can get food for free

foul (FOWL)—an unfair move

free throw (FREE THROH)—a chance at making one point given to someone who has been fouled

locker room (LOK-ur ROOM)—the place where players change into their uniforms

net (NET)—the rope basket that hangs from the rim of the hoop

pledge (PLEJ)—promise to give money

quarter (KWAR-tur)—one section of a basketball game; there are four in each game

record (REK-urd)—highest or best score

sponsor (SPON-sur)—someone who gives money or goods to another person in exchange for advertisement

tournament (TURN-uh-muhnt)—a competition of many different people

1. In this book, many people help Kylie Jean. Who do you think helps the most? Explain your answer.

2. What was the hardest thing Kylie Jean had to do in this book?

3. What do you think happens after this story ends?

Be Creative!

1. Kylie Jean wasn't very good at basketball at the beginning of this book. Write about a time that you tried something you weren't good at. What happened?

2. Who is your favorite character in this story? Draw a picture of that person. Then write a list of five things you know about them.

3. T.J. helped Kylie Jean with free throws. Write about one of your siblings. If you don't have any, write about your best friend. What is something that person does to help you? How do you help them?

This cake was the perfect way to celebrate being the Little Dribbler Queen! Momma and I made it together. Yum-o!

Love, Kylie Jean

From Momma's Kitchen

HOOP QUEEN CAKE

Makes: 1 cake

YOU NEED:

1 box any flavor cake mix

1 can of vanilla frosting

Orange food coloring (or mix yellow and red)

1 tube of chocolate frosting

2 round cake pans

1 toothpick

1 grown-up helper

1. Bake the cake as directed on the box. (Follow the directions for two 10-inch pans.)

2. Let cool.

3. While the cakes cool, mix the vanilla frosting with the food coloring.

4. Once the cakes are cool, put a little frosting on one, and then place the other cake on top of it. (The frosting helps it stay put.)

5. Cover both cakes with the orange frosting.

6. Using the chocolate frosting, draw the basketball's dark lines on top of the orange frosting and around the outside edge of the cake.

7. Serve and enjoy! Yum-o!

Kylie Jean

has one BIG dream . . .
to be a beauty queen!

Available from Picture Window Books
www.capstonepub.com

THE FUN DOESN'T STOP HERE!

Discover more at www.capstonekids.com

- Videos & Contests
- Games & Puzzles
- Friends & Favorites
- Authors & Illustrators

Find cool websites and more books like this one at www.facthound.com. Just type in the Book ID: **9781404859623** and you're ready to go!